DEDICATION

To my wife Coryll,
a fantastic mom...

and to Brady and Brooklyn,
my true inspiration for this story.

ISBN 10: 1-59152-084-3
ISBN 13: 978-1-59152-084-9

Published by Triple Tail Publishing / Randy Rupert

© 2011 by Triple Tail Publishing

Illustrations and design by Robert Rath

sweetgrassbooks
a division of Farcountry Press

Produced by Sweetgrass Books; PO Box 5630, Helena, MT 59604;
(800) 821-3874; www.sweetgrassbooks.com.

Created, produced, and designed in the United States.
Printed in Korea.
December 2011
Pacom, 242-2 Dangjung-dong, Gunpo-si Kyonggi-do, Korea

15 14 13 12 11   1 2 3 4 5 6 7

A DOG-GONE TALE

by Randy Rupert

illustrated by Robert Rath

Triple Tale Publishing

This is a story about three
good friends, three dog friends,
that is! The three friends — a St. Bernard,
a Golden Retriever, and a Poodle — always had so
much fun together, but sometimes they lost their way.

One day, as their parents looked on, Bernie the St. Bernard,
Goldie the Golden Retriever, and Peaches the Poodle played
in a park next to a beautiful forest. It was a sunny day, and they
raced through the park and right to the forest's edge.
"Pay attention," their parents barked. "This is a very busy place.
Don't wander off! We don't want to lose you!"

2

As the day went on the dogs grew dizzy with joy. They kept looking for new things to do! Then Goldie came up with an idea. "Hey! Let's go chase squirrels!" he said, forgetting what his parents had told him earlier in the day.

The three dogs could not resist the fun of chasing those bushy tails! So off they went, running and playing in the trees and bushes.

The forest was a magical place full of squirrels, rabbits, and butterflies.

The puppies splashed in the creek and romped through the flowers.

All of a sudden, Peaches realized it was getting dark in the forest.

"We should get back to the park and find our parents," she said. "But which way did we come? Which path will lead us back?"

The pups looked and
looked, but they
couldn't find their way out
of the forest. They began
to fear they might never
see their parents again.

It was getting as dark as a dog's nose, so they decided to settle near a big tree. Huddling together to stay warm, they vowed to find their way out of the forest in the morning.

That night was the longest of their young lives. The forest that had been so much fun in daylight became a spooky place full of jagged shadows and glowing eyes.

Morning finally came
and Bernie, Goldie,
and Peaches were eager
to find their way out of the
forest and back to their parents
and owners.

They used their special noses to follow
their scent and retrace their steps.
They used their big ears to listen for
the sounds of others playing in the park.

Before they knew it, they
breached the edge of the
forest and ran out into the
park, hoping to jump into
their parents' loving paws.

But they couldn't see
their parents!

The dogs were sad and confused. They wondered what to do next.

After a few minutes of serious thinking, Bernie said, "My owners often take my parents and I to the butcher shop to buy my food. Let's go and see if they are there."

So the three dogs ran through the park, along the river, and over the small bridge.

16

They arrived at the shop and found the butcher. With sad eyes, Bernie whimpered, "Have you seen my parents?"

But the butcher didn't understand dog talk and said, "No, Bernie, I don't have any bones for you today. Do you remember where you buried the last one in the park?"

The little St. Bernard was very sad that the butcher couldn't help him, and the three friends left the store.

Then Goldie had an idea. "My owners often take my parents and I to the sporting goods store to get hunting decoys," he said. "Let's go and see if my parents are there now."

Full of energy again, the dogs raced down the street to the store.

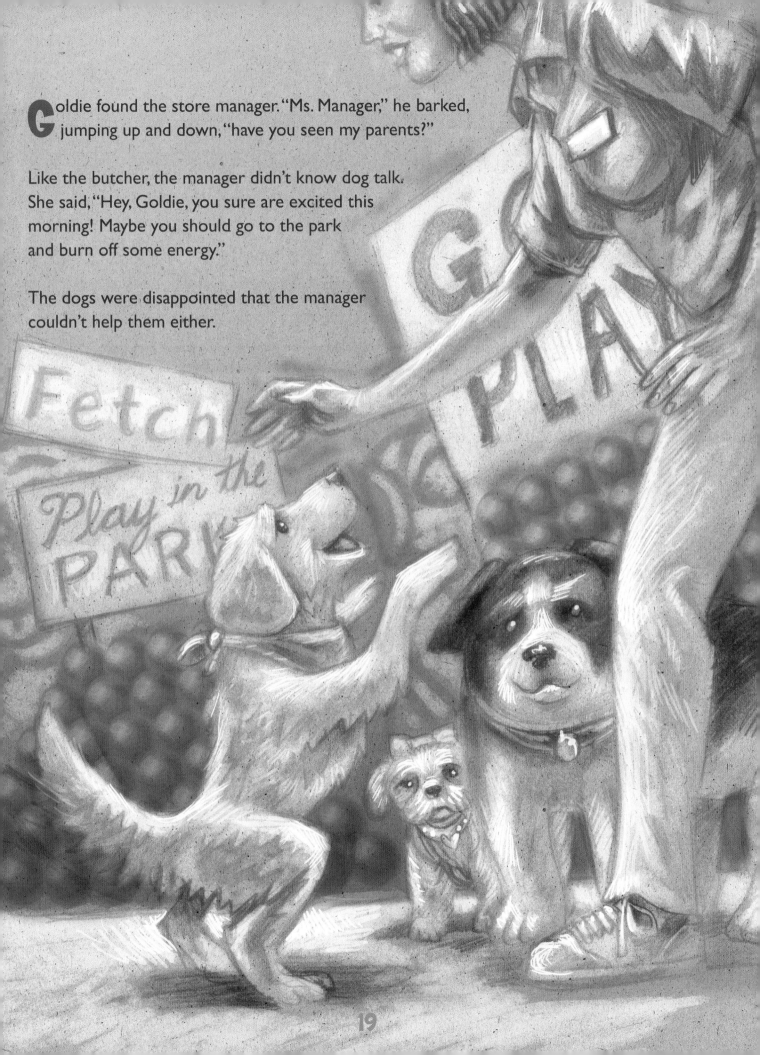

Goldie found the store manager. "Ms. Manager," he barked, jumping up and down, "have you seen my parents?"

Like the butcher, the manager didn't know dog talk. She said, "Hey, Goldie, you sure are excited this morning! Maybe you should go to the park and burn off some energy."

The dogs were disappointed that the manager couldn't help them either.

Now Peaches was really worried. She asked,
"Where could my mommy be? Maybe she
has an appointment at the beauty salon to trim
her fur and shine her nails."

Bernie and Goldie thought this made sense,
so they raced over to the Grooming Salon.

They arrived at the beauty shop
and ran up to the salon manager.

"Peaches! What a surprise!" the groomer
squealed. "You aren't scheduled for a
makeover until next week. I'm afraid you'll
have to wait until then to show everyone
at the park how pretty you are."

Once again, the dogs were sad
that no one could help them.

They sat on the sidewalk and tried to figure out why their people friends couldn't help them.

"I don't want to dig up my bones at the park.
I just want to find my parents," said Bernie.

"And I don't need playtime at the park," said Goldie.
"I need my mom and dad."

"And I certainly don't want to show off my new look at the park," Peaches sniffed. "I just want to look for my mommy!"

As they wondered how they were
going to find their parents, the answer
slowly came to them...

They looked at each other and said at the
same time, "We should go back to where
we first lost our parents...THE PARK!"

Zig-zagging through bikers and joggers, they ran back to the park as fast as they could.

As the three best friends rounded
a bend, they couldn't believe their eyes!
Gathered at the park were not only their
owners, but best of all... their PARENTS!

They barked and leaped right into the safety of their parents' paws! Their parents were so happy and relieved to find their pups safe and sound.

On the way home, Mr. and Mrs. Bernard, Mr. and Mrs. Retriever, and Mr. and Mrs. Poodle all had a talk with their little ones. They talked about the importance of listening to rules and making the right choices.

The three dogs learned a valuable lesson that day— and they promised never to wander away from their parents again.

ABOUT THE AUTHOR

Randy Rupert was raised in Montana and has spent years working in business sales and marketing. But no deal has ever compared to the experience of writing his first book and creating a lasting memory for his son and daughter.

When his son was 3, Randy created the "Dog Story" to help teach him the importance of staying with his parents in a way he'd understand. His son's love of the story is what drove Randy to recreate it in print. Randy hopes it will help other parents teach a valuable lesson while having fun with their children like he did with his son.

DOG-GONE

ACKNOWLEDGMENTS

When writing my first book, I came to realize just how many people are so very important in having an impact on the development of a story.

First, I would like to thank Kathy Springmeyer for her hours of conversation, advice, and direction in helping this very naïve new author find his way. I could not have begun this journey without her.

Second, to Robert Rath, an unbelievable talent in both creativity and artistry, these dogs would not have come alive without his caring hand. Thanks, Robert, let's create something fun again soon!

Third, to Gayle Shirley, who carefully made this new author's words flow smoothly, so this story would help it's pictures speak to each and every young child. Thanks, Gayle.

Fourth, to my parents, Keith and Nancy, and my family, who always make me believe that you have a very good chance of accomplishing your dreams if you are passionate and driven about the dream.

And most importantly, to my loving and encouraging wife Coryll, who told me many years ago to write down the story I told my son nightly.